Jennifer Moore-Mallinos
Andy Catling

What Would YOU Do...

Loyola Press.

Contents

- Help Her Cheat? 4
- $20, Found! 6
- Being Bullied 8
- Dirty Face 10
- A Tricky Stranger 12
- Something New for Dinner 14
- New Hairstyle 16
- One Piece of Pizza Left 18
- Your Dog Pooped 20
- Not Enough Money 22
- Mean Message 24
- Website Surfing 26
- Borrowed Without Asking 28
- Lost Dog 30
- Birthday Party 32
- Teasing 34
- Scared 36
- Mom's Medicine 38
- Got to Go Pee 40
- Stranger at the Door 42
- Dog Wants My Dinner 44
- Telephone Eavesdropping 46
- Toothache 48
- Ripped Pants 50

- Feelings 52
- Broken Bottles 54
- Yucky Medicine 56
- Food Fight 58
- To Lie or Not to Lie 60
- Freezer Door Ajar 62
- Unsafe Secrets 64
- Seat Belt Troubles 66
- Garbage Disposal Dilemma 68
- Really Mad 70
- Hide-and-Seek 72
- The Traveling Toilet Paper 74
- Biting Brother 76
- Forgotten Homework 78
- "You're Fat!" 80
- "He Won't Wake Up!" 82
- Math Test 84
- Your Neighbor's Pink Roses 86
- Finger in the Fan 88
- Singing in the Choir 90
- Hiding in the Clothes Rack 92
- Found a Lighter 94

What would you do if your friend asked you to **help her cheat** on her science test?

Would you help her or would you ask her if she needed help studying so that she didn't have to cheat?

Sometimes when we are afraid of not doing well, we look for ways to make things easier, even if it means cheating. Consider asking your friend what was making her so nervous about the test and then ask if she wants you to help her study.

Sometimes having a friend's help is all you need.

What would you do if you saw a $20 bill fall out of a person's pocket when you were walking behind her?

Would you keep the money or would you give it back?

It would be tempting to keep the money, but it would not be the right thing to do. The right thing to do would be to pick up the money and give it back to the person who dropped it.

One day you might need someone to do the same for you.

What would you do if your friend told you he was **being bullied** at school and wanted you to keep it a secret?

Would you keep it a secret OR would you ask a teacher for help?
Asking an adult for help is OK. Keeping a secret about a friend who is getting hurt is not a good secret to keep.

Remember, safety first because it does matter!

What would you do if your brother had **ketchup all** over his face when he was eating a hamburger?

Would you ignore it or would you hand him a napkin so he could wipe his face?
There's nothing worse than having something on your face and nobody telling you. Wouldn't you want somebody to help you? Helping somebody else is the right thing to do.

Especially when it's your brother.

Would you go with him $\mathcal{Or}$ not?
Going anywhere with a stranger, especially when you are alone, is not a good idea. It is not safe! The stranger is a stranger and that means that you don't know if he or she is nice or not.

So to be on the safe side, don't go!

What would you do if you went to your **aunt's house** and she made something for dinner that you'd never had before and

it didn't look that yummy?

Would you tell your aunt that the dinner looked yucky or would you try a little?
Consider taking a bite. When somebody works hard to make you something, it's polite to try it. Sometimes it's hard trying something new, but you might surprise yourself and learn that you really like it!

So give it a try! Yum!

What would you do if your mom just got a **new hairstyle** that you didn't really like, but then she asks you if you like it?

Would you tell her that her new hairstyle looks terrible or would you smile and tell her that she looks beautiful no matter what kind of hairstyle she has? Telling somebody something that you know will make them sad can sometimes be avoided.

Can you think of a time when you were careful not to hurt another person's feelings?

Would you take the last piece and quickly gobble it all up or would you share it with your friend?

Sharing is always a good thing to do! Just remember how good it felt the last time somebody shared something with you. That's the same feeling other people get when you share with them.

It feels great!

Would you stop and pick up the poop or would you quickly walk away?

Keeping our neighborhood clean means picking up after our pets. It's not that fun to do, but it's part of being a responsible pet owner. So the next time you go for a walk with your dog, don't forget to bring a bag.

Just in case!

What would you do if you went to the store and you saw something that you really, **really wanted** but you didn't have enough money to buy it?

Would you take it or would you work extra hard to save your money so that you could buy it later?

Yikes! Taking something that you did not pay for is stealing, and stealing is not OK. It can be hard sometimes having to wait to buy something that you want, but you can do it! A little hard work never hurt anybody!

Is there something that you really want to buy?

What would you do if your friend dared you to send a **mean message** on your phone to one of the other kids at school?

Would you send the message or lose the dare?

Losing the dare is the right thing to do. Any game that hurts other people is not a good game to play because making other people feel bad is not fun.

It's called bullying!

What would you do if you were at school and one of the other kids in your computer class showed you how to go on to a **website** that was not meant for kids?

Would you go on to the website or would you tell him NO?

It's OK to tell another person not to do something. If they don't listen to you, then it's time to ask a grown-up for help. A true friend would never ask you to do something that they knew was wrong.

But it's up to you to say NO.

What would you do if you **borrowed** your sister's pants without asking permission and then you accidentally ripped them?

Would you put the pants back in her closet without telling her or would you tell her the truth, even though you know she will get mad at you?

It can be hard to tell the truth about something that you did wrong. But it's the right thing to do, especially when you know that the truth is going to come out eventually. Sooner or later, your sister would take her pants out of the closet to wear them.

And see the hole!

What would you do if you found a **lost dog**?

Would you pretend you didn't see it and walk away or would you try to help the dog by finding its owner?

Remember, it's never a good idea to go near a dog you don't know. First, tell your mom or dad about the dog. Then with mom or dad's help, look to see if the dog has a tag with his name and address.

Being lost is scary!

What would you do if you were invited to your friend's **birthday party**, but you don't like some of the other kids that are going to be at the party?

Would you tell your friend that you couldn't go or would you go to the party anyway?
Just think how sad your friend would be if you didn't go. You don't have to like everybody, but that shouldn't stop you from having fun.

And besides, you might be surprised and find out that the other kids are not that bad after all!

What would you do if your friends kept **teasing** you because you like to dance ballet?

Would you stop ballet dancing or would you keep dancing because it's something you really like to do?

Dance! Doing things that you like is important and fun. And even though it can be hard to ignore your friends sometimes, it doesn't matter what they think. It matters that you're doing what you love.

What is something you like to do for fun?

What would you do if you didn't want to go to school because you were **scared** of taking a spelling test?

Would you pretend you were sick so that you could stay home *or* would you try your best to be ready for the test?

Getting ready for a test at school can be scary! The best thing you can do is to practice, practice, practice.

And don't forget it's OK to ask for help if you need it.

What would you do if you saw your **mom's medicine** sitting on the counter in the bathroom?

Would you pick it up and try to open it or would you leave it alone and walk away?
It's never safe to touch or try to take somebody else's medicine. The only medicine we should take is the medicine the doctor gives us.

And only when mom or dad says it's OK.

What would you do if you were having a lot of **fun swimming** in the pool

and suddenly you had to pee

Would you go pee in the pool or would you quickly get out of the pool and go to the bathroom?

Yuck! Peeing in the pool is not healthy and can make others sick! So take a few minutes and do what you have to do.

Don't worry, the pool will still be there when you get back.

What would you do if a stranger came to your house and **knocked** on the door?

Would you open the door and let him or her in or would you wait for your mom or dad?
The safest thing to do if a stranger comes to your door is to wait for your mom or dad. That way they can decide whether or not to open the door.

Remember, strangers may look nice but you don't really know if they are nice!

What would you do if you were eating **dinner** and your dog wanted to have a taste?

Would you give him just a little taste or would you give him a dog biscuit instead?
It's hard to say NO to our furry friends when they look so cute, but giving your pet people food is not always good for him.

Instead give him a doggy treat. He will love it!

What would you do if you picked up the **telephone** and heard your sister talking to her friend?

Would you sit quietly and listen to their conversation or would you hang up the phone?

Hang up the phone. Listening in on other people's conversations is not a good idea.

Maybe they are talking about something private.

What would you do if you had a **toothache** and you were scared to tell your mom because

you don't like going to the dentist

Would you pretend it didn't hurt *or* would you tell your mom that you had a toothache?

Going to the dentist is not much fun, but it is worse to be in pain. The only way your mom or dad can help you when you are hurt is if you tell them.

It's OK, you can do it!

What would you do if your friend fell down and got **mud** on her pants?

Would you laugh at her *or* would you help her up and make sure she's OK?

It never feels good when somebody laughs at you, especially when you are hurt and feel embarrassed. The best thing to do is to first make sure your friend is not hurt. Then tell her that she has mud on her pants so that she can put on a new pair.

How would you feel if somebody laughed at you?

What would you do if you felt really, really sad?

Would you keep your feelings all closed up inside you or would you talk to somebody, like your mom or dad, about how you were feeling? Sometimes talking about your feelings can be hard, but not talking about your feelings can be even harder. Did you know that not only will you feel better after talking about what is making you sad, but you might be able to make things better by solving the problem.

Share your feelings with somebody who you trust.

What would you do if you were at the park and you found **broken bottles** scattered on the playground?

Would you pick up the broken pieces of glass or would you keep playing on the playground anyway?

Neither! It is nice to want to clean up the playground, but picking up pieces of broken glass can be dangerous. It is never a good idea to play in an area full of broken glass.

The best thing to do is to ask a trusted adult you know for help.

What would you do if you were sick and the doctor gave you medicine that tasted really, really yucky?

Would you moan and complain, hoping that you wouldn't have to take the medicine or would you take the medicine so that you could get better?

It's never fun being sick. And sometimes we have to do things we don't want to do. Taking terrible-tasting medicine is one of them. So be brave, open wide, and count to three.

Before you know it, you will be feeling better!

What would you do if you were at school in the cafeteria and one of the kids yelled "Food Fight!" and started to throw food?

Would you join in or would you walk away?

It might be hard to walk away when the food fight looks like a lot of fun, but just think of the big mess afterward. And what a waste of food!

Food is meant to be eaten, not played with!

What would you do if you really wanted to go to the movies with your friend, but you thought your mom and dad wouldn't let you?

Do you tell your mom and dad that you're going to a friend's house, but you really go to the movies instead OR do you ask to go to the movies with your friend and hope for the best?

Yikes! Telling your parents that you are at one place when you're really at another is dangerous. Not only is that lying, but it's not safe. Our parents need to know where we are and who we are with at all times. Maybe if they dropped you off and picked you up after the movie, they would let you go.

Where do you have to ask permission to go?

What would you do if you left the **freezer door** open and all the ice cream started to melt?

Would you blame it on your younger brother or would you confess and tell the truth?

Blame it on your brother—just joking! It wasn't like you left the freezer door open on purpose. It was a mistake! So the best thing to do—even though it might be hard—is to take responsibility and say you are sorry.

Then to make things even better, help clean up all the melted ice cream.

What would you do if one of the kids at your school made you feel **unsafe** or **uncomfortable**?

Would you keep it a secret because the kid told you to *or* would you tell a grown-up you know and trust? This kind of secret is an unsafe secret and that means that you need to tell an adult like your teacher or your mom or dad. Remember, not all secrets are OK to keep.

Asking a grown-up for help is the right thing to do!

What would you do if you were riding in the car and your **seat belt** was too tight?

Would you undo your seat belt but pretend you were still wearing it or would you ask for help?
Safety always comes first, especially when you're riding in a car. Maybe there is a reason your seatbelt is too tight, and you'll only have to do something easy like taking off your big, thick coat to make your seatbelt fit better.

Where else do you wear a seat belt?

Would you stick your hand down the disposal to try to reach the spoon or would you walk away and pretend it didn't happen?

Neither! It is never OK to put your hand in a garbage disposal. It's too dangerous. Not telling anybody that there is a spoon in the disposal is also dangerous. The best thing to do is tell your mom or dad what happened.

Then they can get the spoon out of the disposal safely.

What would you do if you were really, **really mad** at your best friend?

Would you yell and scream at her or would you try to relax first by taking three deep breaths before you tell your friend how you're feeling?

It's OK to be mad, but it's what you do when you're mad that matters. Yelling and screaming never helps solve a problem. Before you can talk about your feelings, you first need to calm down. Taking three deep breaths can really help.

How do you calm down when you're mad?

What would you do if you were playing **hide-and-seek** and one of your friends thought climbing to the top of a very tall tree was a good place to hide?

Would you cheer him on to keep climbing or would you tell him to stop climbing because it wasn't safe?

Trying to find the best hiding place so you can't be found is fun when you are playing a game of hide-and-seek. Hiding in a place that is not safe is not a good idea. Climbing up high in a tree might seem OK on your way up. But don't forget, eventually you have to climb down. That could be very scary.

It's OK to have fun, but safety always comes first!

Would you pretend you didn't see it and say nothing or would you tell him?

Sometimes when other kids are unkind to us we want to be unkind back to them, but that doesn't make it right. Quietly telling someone that they have toilet paper stuck to their shoe is the right thing to do. No matter who it is would be happy and relieved that he was not embarrassed in front of other kids.

Has anybody ever helped you so that you didn't feel embarrassed?

What would you do if your **little brother** came up to you and bit you really hard on your arm?

Would you bite him back or would you try to teach him that biting is not OK?
Biting him back might be the first thing you want to do, but it's not the right thing. The right thing to do is to stop, take a deep breath, and then tell him what other things he could bite.

Can you think of some things that are OK for a little guy to bite instead of biting you?

What would you do if your teacher gave you **a note** to give to your parents that you knew was about homework you never turned in

Would you "forget" to give your parents the note *or* would you give your parents the note and hope they don't freak out?

Forgetting to give your parents the note might get you into bigger trouble. It's best to give your parents the note and also let them know that you plan to finish your homework and turn it in to your teacher.

Don't forget, it's always OK to ask for help, especially when it comes to getting your homework done.

What do you do to make sure you get your homework done?

What would you do if your best friend called you "fat"?

Would you stop eating and try to lose weight or would you tell your friend that what she said was not very nice and that she hurt your feelings?

It is never a good choice to stop eating. Telling your friend how you feel about what she said IS a good choice.

Smile! You're Beautiful!

What would you do if you came home from school and you found your older brother **sleeping** facedown on the floor and, no matter how hard you tried, he wouldn't wake up?

Would you just leave him and walk away or would you get help?
That would be scary! You definitely need to get help!

What can you do when you need help?

What would you do if your friend asked you to show her your answers during a **math test**?

Would you let your friend look at your paper or would you ignore her?
Helping your friend is a nice thing to do, but helping her cheat on a test is never a good idea.

What else could you do to help your friend?

What would you do if it was your grandma's birthday and her favorite thing in the whole wide world is **pink roses**, and your neighbor grows pink roses in her garden

Would you sneak over to your neighbor's yard when nobody was home and cut a few roses to give to your grandma or would you wait until your neighbor got home and ask her permission?

It is always better to ask for something you want rather than just taking it. You might be surprised to learn that by simply asking nicely for something, you might just get it!

You never know unless you ask!

Would you stick your finger in the fan or not?

Yikes! Sticking your finger or anything else into a fan is not safe!

It could cut your finger badly if you did that!

What would you do if you were **singing in the choir**, in front of the whole school, and all of a sudden you felt like you were going to throw up?

Would you keep singing, hoping to feel better soon *or* would you leave quietly and go to the bathroom?

This is a tough one! It might be hard to tell if your tummy hurts because you're nervous or if you're getting sick. Either way, it might be best to take a few minutes to find out. Just imagine what might happen if you threw up in the middle of a song!

Sometimes it's better to stop what you're doing and make sure everything is all right.

What would you do if you went shopping with your mom and, while your mom was busy looking at the dresses, your little brother decided it would be **fun to hide** behind the clothes racks at the store?

Would you say nothing and let your brother keep hiding or **would you tell your mom?**
Little kids think it's fun to hide or explore, especially when they are getting bored. But it wouldn't be fun if he got lost. So, telling your mom is the better idea. That way she can keep your brother with her.

Or maybe you could be her helper and hold your brother's hand.

Would you pick it up and try to make it work *or* would you leave it alone?

Playing with matches or a lighter is very dangerous! Not only could you get hurt, but you could also start a fire.

Matches and lighters are for grown-ups to use, not kids!

LoyolaPress.

3441 N. Ashland Avenue
Chicago, Illinois 60657
(800) 621-1008
www.loyolapress.com

Text: Jennifer Moore-Mallinos
Illustration: Andy Catling
Design and layout: Estudi Guasch, S.L.
© Gemser Publications, S.L. 2019
El Castell, 38 08329 Teià (Barcelona, Spain)
www.mercedesros.com
Published in the United States in 2020 by Loyola Press.
ISBN: 978-0-8294-5013-2
Library of Congress Control Number: 2020932308
Printed in China.

All rights reserved. No part of this book may be reproduced in any form, by photostat, microfilm, xerography, or any other means, or incorporated into any information retrieval system, electronic or mechanical, without the written permission of the copyright owner.